HIT

J.N. Razic

MINERVA PRESS
LONDON
MIAMI DELHI SYDNEY

ISBN 0 75411 010 9

First Published 2000 by
MINERVA PRESS
315–317 Regent Street
London W1R 7YB

Printed in Great Britain for Minerva Press

HIT

To Kay, Steve,
Tracy, Dawn and
Wayne
from
JNR.

Death of a Centurion

He slipped on his shaded lenses and braved the street lights. His appetite was tickled; his hunger grew ravenous by the second as he sensed the prey in the night. Friday, Saturday, Sunday: the nights of hunting, four days had gone since his last hit, and now that had worn off, his frame felt weakened and weakness was his downfall. The skin round his fingernails began to itch severely. He rubbed skin cream around them to ease the uncomfortable itch. He needed a hit desperately, or he would tear himself apart in a fit of violence.

He tried to keep in with the fashions of the night, but didn't want to be too original. He had to keep unnoticed – just a face in the crowds.

He dismissed his usual hit zones, casually walking past them, ignoring the bouncers' gaze, his mental map looking over the list of clubs he had been to so far, searching for something new. He had been to a large majority of them, becoming accustomed to their layouts, the areas and corners where the best hits lay, hanging out until the early hours when they would occasionally stray on to the dance floor. They would stay there, almost waiting for him, summoned by him unknowingly... and then be drained dry by him. But he was becoming recognised now, his tinted lenses giving him away; whenever he was asked about them he would reply that they were a fashion accessory. But they had a more important function than that. There were still a lot of clubs he had not hunted in before; a couple of gay bars and clubs. The first one he came to was called Centurions. He passed the bouncers casually, acting calm as he entered into his hunting ground, even though the hunger raged inside him.

He drew looks from the male clientele as he passed them, aiming for the bar. He ordered himself a mineral water.

The barman was confused, taken aback; this client looked like a hard drinker. He could usually tell between soft and hard drinkers. The shaded client gave him a red-lensed stare which seemed to last for minutes until he said, 'People are not always what they seem to be.'

The barman took a step back and accepted the money he was handed; the thought that the shaded customer had read his mind disturbed him. The client took his change and turned away, lights reflecting off his red lenses.

He loved using his mental powers on unsuspecting people, psyching them out. It was his second pleasure in life. Then he sensed it…

'I'm Richard.'

He turned round and looked over the newcomer. Possibly cocaine; taken before he came here, to boost his self-confidence before coming here. He had a girlfriend, but was a closet gay and now relaxed with the people he was surrounded by. The slight accent sounded American or Canadian. He worked for some successful international firm, with a cigar-wielding boss. He had escaped the bonds of routine life for one night: no more lies.

'Good evening,' he replied, staring deep into Richard's eyes.

'I like the glasses,' Richard said over the music.

'I have damaged retinas,' he replied. It was no lie. It got a powerful sympathy vote from some people. Like this one.

After half an hour's barely audible talk under the

pounding bass they left, Richard inviting him back to his place, a flat in the rich area of town.

He had been right. It was the flat of an executive. Even had a picture of his girlfriend on a corner table next to his mobile phone. How careless, he thought.

'Would you like a drink?'

He turned and looked at Richard. He was nervous, this would be his first time he had brought his feelings to the surface, to reality.

He had never had a gay as a hit before. There was a first time for everything. He felt his fingernails itch again and tried to control himself. Control. Control... He felt a twinge of pity for Richard; but only a twinge. His need was far greater.

'Yes, please. Do you have any mineral water?'

'I'm afraid not. I'm out at the moment.'

Then Richard violently embraced him and kissed him hard on the lips. All the desire poured out, all the years of repression, the hidden homosexual nature, the buried love, were gone; only his true love existed now.

The moment Richard kissed him, he felt the stiff needles grow from beneath his fingernails and search out Richard's neck, and find the area in which to inject his fluid. His mind's powers joined Richard's and started to drain the cocaine effects from his mind. Wherever the drug lay he would find it. All his hit was left with was a few moments of ecstatic pleasure – then death.

Richard moaned in pleasure as the needles entered him and the fluid mixed in him, the stranger's mind sucking his own mind dry of chemical pleasure. Then he blew his mind.

Chapter One

Wake up in Bedlam

Dex lay on the bed, covers scattered everywhere, when he heard the key in the front door. His sister was home. Mum would do her nut. He heard his mum come out of her bedroom. Then the barrage started.

He pulled the covers back over his head and tried to block out the row downstairs. He hated these mornings. He had college to go to, but had to get out of the house before Mum started on him too with questions. The papers had been full of stories about teenagers hooked on heroin and dying from Ecstasy and now his mother feared for her children ending up on a life-support machine or in a rehab clinic.

Dex never touched drugs. Only once, when he took a toke of a joint at a party, but that was it. To have a good time, he had a few lagers, a race in his car with his mates, and a willing girl. But Lou, his sister, did drugs. He knew the signs. He knew people at college who were at it – the party stuff, the heighteners.

His mother had a right to worry.

★

He opened the door to his flat, his hunger satisfied. His hit had died, his mind blown away in a halluci-nightmare, believing he had been drowned in a vat of cocaine, choking to death on the white powder as his girlfriend and boss forced his head down further into it, muttering 'Faggot' and 'Coke-head' at him poisonously. When the police found the body they would come to the obvious conclusion: overdose. But not cocaine. He left out a bowl full of cocaine on Richard's table; the coke he had found in Richard's bathroom cabinet. The overdose would be something chemical and fluid – his fluid.

He had been tempted to take the coke and use it for himself, but the idea of snorting or injecting if it was some other drug made his stomach turn. He did not need these barbaric methods. He had been born with these stiff fleshy needles for that whole purpose, and his mental powers were able to take the psychological effects from his victims.

He would need another few hits, though, at least until his next hunting period. He was running out of clubs to stalk and considered it was soon to be time to move city again, and search out new victims.

He made himself a cup of iced lemon tea and rested, feeling Richard's drug surge through his body, invigorating him once again.

★

Lou changed and got out of the house before she said something to her mother she would later regret. It was unfair; Dex went out and came home late and never had to suffer the inquisition she suffered this morning. She had only stayed at a friend's house; it was not as if she had been sleeping rough or selling herself on the streets. She could not have found out about the Ecstasy she had taken. Not even Dex knew. It was all because she was the youngest of the family, and her mum's only daughter.

Mum made herself a cup of coffee laced with whisky to calm herself and sat on the sofa. What was happening with her daughter? If she was staying over somewhere, why didn't she phone and explain? Her only hope was that Dex did not turn down his sister's rocky path. And to make things worse, she was taking drugs.

Dex parked his souped-up Escort and made his way up the college steps, which seemed dull and unwelcome at this time in the morning, dampened by the rain. He was half asleep and would probably drop off during studies. Why he'd chosen computer studies was beyond him.

Chapter Two

World Seen Red

He could start to feel his arm tingle now. The hit was wearing off a little. It was not serious, but another hit tonight and one tomorrow would sort him out for the coming week.

It was not only his victims that suffered nightmares; he himself was subjected to them while he was asleep. It was a recurring nightmare about himself, about his birth into this world. But it was no dream; it was real, a memory he wanted to forget but could not. Sometimes he felt almost like he was the only one of his kind, stalking the cities for the narcotic food that kept him alive. He tried once abstaining from the draining of drugs. He lasted two weeks. He was practically half dead, a withered walking thing, but then he came across some junkies on derelict ground while he staggered home dying. He fed on them for hours, regaining his strength and vitality. Since then he'd realised that he needed it to survive. He learnt in his fledgling years that to live such an existence in this body you had to destroy all emotions. You had to be sexless. No mercy, no remorse. He was an animal, killing to survive. If his victims died while he drained them then it was bad luck. It was like life – you win or you lose.

This morning he dreamt again: the Dream, the Nightmare. The nightmare that haunted him from his birth. His mother lay on the bed, her legs in stirrups, her belly pregnant, buzzing with new life. Doctors were there, also others, men in suits with face masks on. Mother had been a junkie; she hadn't just taken heroin, but anything she could lay her hands on, like her mother, and her mother before. They were a family of addicts. Father had been an alcoholic. He was violent, so he had been told. He died an alcoholic, his liver shrivelled, his stomach bloated, his mind gone. The suited men knew that; they wanted to know what the babies would turn out like, being the next generation down from a family of addicts. The scanner had shown twins. They would watch, fascinated.

He heard her scream as he slipped out into the world of glaring lights, illuminating them, and saw the faces hidden by surgical masks. He saw every detail through quickly developing eyesight. Something slipped out beside him aided by the doctor's gloved hands.

Umbilical cords were cut. He knew he was special; he knew that the people who stood around him looked down in wonder and awe. He looked beside him and saw the other fleshy form like himself. It did not move. His mother screamed, cutting through his cries and the voices of the men who observed. It was a cry of pain and despair, piercing his sensitive ears. Now he was hearing more and more, knowing the other child was dead.

'What is this…?' the doctor asked, shocked. The suited men said nothing. They were pleasantly surprised.

'Mother…' he said, through forming vocal cords, lips corresponding to the words. His words were directed at the woman whose legs he lay between.

'It *talks*,' someone muttered behind his mask.

'They're freaks!' cried one, ripping away his surgical mask and storming out of the delivery room.

The strong lights started to burn his sensitive eyes painfully, so he snuggled up to one of his mother's thighs and shielded his eyes.

His mother moaned and lay silent.

★

He awoke, his skin crawling, exuding sweat, his fingers itching painfully. He groaned, writhing in sweat-soaked sheets.

'Mother...' he moaned, sobs catching in his throat.

He opened his eyes, daylight stinging them through a gap in the curtains. He reached out and swiped his lenses from the bedside table and put them on, to see a crimson dagger spear the wall.

He would wait until night again, to fill the pit where the hunger had now settled and started to grow again, gnawing away, micro-bite by micro-bite.

He had no job. The company the suited men worked for paid him a lot of compensation for the experiments they conducted on him while he grew up. He would never need to work in his life. His neighbours wondered how a person could live in such an expensive flat and have no known employment. When they enquired, he lied about having some industrial accident which affected his sight – hence the shaded lenses. But he knew they formed their own ideas about him, not through fear, but paranoid curiosity. It did not bother him; he did not need them. They did not have to worry, as no addicts lived in his neighbourhood.

But living day by day, year after year, on his own lonely crusade to remain alive, made him yearn for a companion, someone like himself, with the same need, the same hunger, the same craving for a hit. His opposite: the ying to his yang. There had been one once – the tiny form born only moments after himself. It had died, along with his mother, on his birthday. He recalled the words he was taunted with while in the care of the company that was interested in him, that experimented on him: he was a 'freak', an abomination on this earth, a chemical result, not human. These words would burn in his memory forever – spears of mental torment.

He had no parents, no brothers or sisters. Often he considered suicide, but he was made of stronger stuff. He decided to live, and not die by his own choice. He would live and hopefully sire a child, a normal child – not some born junkie like himself – and then die, being the last of his kind.

As a tear of pain rolled down his cheek he banished all pity for the human race. Since humans lived off raping the earth and nature, he would live off the human and its chemical vices.

★

'What do you say?'

Dex awoke from his slight doze as he sat, slumped in a chair in the common room or 'chill-out room' as the students preferred to call it.

'Zeppelins.'

'Zeppelins?'

'You haven't heard? Most of us are going on Saturday.'

'What's Zeppelins?'

'Zeppelins? It's the best rave club in town,' Neil explained, trying to coax the money out of Dex's pocket, 'and I have tickets.'

'How the fuck did you buy tickets when you still owe me forty quid?'

'Well…' Neil replied, making a pained face.

'No, I don't.'

'Listen, there'll be girls, drugs…' he went on, trying to lure the money out of Dex's pocket like a snake charmer.

'I don't do drugs,' said Dex, trying to get comfy in his seat. 'And if you had any sense you wouldn't touch that shit, either. Take up driving. Speed, that's a natural drug – better than that chemical shit I've seen you take. Do you know what that stuff's doing to your body?'

'You sound like my parents. Well, girls then – you touch them.'

I do more than just touch them, Dex reflected, thinking back to the night before in the supermarket car park, and his willing girl.

'Well, what do you say?' asked a despairing Neil.

'And what about my money?'

'As soon as I sell the tickets I can pay you back.'

Some chance, thought Dex.

'Well…?'

Dex just wanted to go to sleep.

Meanwhile Lou sat in the centre of town with one of her old classmates from her last school, idling away the boredom of unemployment. Her mother always went on about how Dex had the right idea about going to college. Dex was perfect in her mother's eyes, but she knew from one of her friends that Dex's sexual behaviour would one day send him to an AIDS clinic. She was dreading the result of his nocturnal activities in the back of his car and behind pubs. It was not that she didn't want a job – she would love the money; but at her age of seventeen her wage would be peanuts, and what she wanted to do was have fun.

'What do you say, then?' asked Justine, her fellow unemployed fun-lover.

'About Zeppelins? I don't know yet. I should be able to; my Giro comes through tomorrow.'

'We don't have to spend that much, and I've bought your ticket as a birthday present, anyway. And I know somebody who can get some stuff, and for a very cheap price,' she explained, opening her can of Coke and watching it froth up and spill on to her jeans. 'Fuck!' was her only response.

They moved off towards the high street and window shopped, dreaming of the day when they would meet their millionaire boyfriends with money to throw to the wind.

'I will, then. Mum will have to wait for her board money,' Lou declared.

'*Board money*! Your mum makes you pay board money, when you're on the dole?'

Lou found Justine's reaction hurtful, but she did not know much about her family really anyway; the problems, Dad…

'I've got to get out, Jus. Mum's driving me crazy. And "ever-so-perfect" Dex is no help, either.'

'Your Dex is a boring bastard anyway. I hope he crashes his car and his knob drops off with overuse!'

Lou laughed and almost spilt her carton of fast-food fries. But laughter did not come easily to her today. She had been waiting all week for this day. Her pregnancy tester had shown positive, and in a few hours' time she would be at the doctor's finding out the results of the tests the doctor had done. She was too young to be pregnant.

★

He stepped out into the daylight, the warmth of the sun making his skin crawl with pleasure. He needed money, and a new shirt for the evening.

He looked less conspicuous now with his lenses on in the brightness of the sun; he often received strange looks from people when he wore them under clouded skies and dirty white snow.

He would often look out into the crowds of people through his red-tinted vision, and wonder how many addicts lay out there in the busy shopping arcades just waiting to be drained by him… addicts worshipping their vice as a means of survival in the rigours of the everyday world. Whether it was narcotics, alcohol, sex or even chocolate, addicts were all the same. There was no legal or illegal, he thought, only the way a country's law was written. But who ever said law was fair?

He closed his thought processes and entered a throng of shoppers in the afternoon brightness – a normal, everyday person.

Chapter Three

Highway Chaser

Dex felt the last of the lager empty from the bottle and slip down his throat while he groped for his car keys in his pocket. The girl whom he stood with looked up at him like he was a dream come true. She was in love. His mates were drinking up and getting ready for some buzzing behind the wheels of their cars. Dex was fired up in his guts and snaked an arm round the girl's slim waist, clasping her thin, brightly coloured dress that shimmered in the lighting of the pub.

'Are we off, then?' she asked giddily.

He started to kiss her and she did not stop him, turning submissive to his assertiveness. He pulled away.

'We'll be off, then.'

They went out into the car park and got into his car, slipping on to the covered seats. It was dark outside and the streets seemed silent.

'You can put your seat belt on if you want,' he said, danger flashing in his eyes. She did; he didn't.

He revved his engine, and waited for the others to go, exhausts exhaling black pollution. He followed them out, tyres screaming, catching up with them, the needle on his speed gauge rising. He pushed in a tape into his radio/tape deck and turned up the volume until it rattled his windows. The girl didn't seemed bothered by it all. She had been in many cars like this, been with many drivers like this. But this was no ordinary driver, thought Dex, this was a speed freak.

He had already passed Mick – 'Driver One'; and now Lee – 'Driver Two' – was in his sights. Approaching fast, he changed up a gear and started to overtake with his tyres burning rubber. He was almost past Lee when another car came into view, a horn blared and Dex slowed and swung back so quick it lifted him out of his seat.

'Shit!'

He looked sideways at the girl. If she was afraid, she did not show it. In fact her legs seemed to part, and a look of excitement showed on her face. Speed and vibrations. That was the speed freak's aphrodisiac. She was one too. Definitely.

He opened the windows and felt the wind enter. He turned his attention back to Lee, 'Driver Two'. He put his foot down and overtook him, screaming past, the wind blowing the girl's hair all over the place.

'*Fuck you!*' he screamed at the top of his voice, leaving Lee, 'Driver Two', in his wake. His heart beat furiously. He was ready for anything. The girl had better be prepared for him. He was past the point of no return; his blood was up. He was switched on, full blast.

Frankie, 'Driver Three', was now in his sights. The lager was now buzzing around his head and he felt the steering wheel start to slip from his sweaty hands. It was only sweat. Sweat from the adrenaline rush he was experiencing. He was catching him. He could see the approaching traffic lights ahead. Green. Frankie went through, Dex chasing his distant tail lights. Don't change! He was almost there.

Then it happened.

Amber.

'*Fuck!*'

He dropped gears and stamped on the brake but he was going too fast and his balding tyres were not gripping the road. He had to go through. The red light blazed into his mind and rubber burned, gears crashed as he went through and a lorry loomed up at his side, approaching the other way, hurtling towards the side of his slowing car.

'Fuck! Fuck! Fuck!'

The lorry driver's horn screamed in his ears and the car juddered as the lorry just avoided him. He was past the lights now, and picking up speed again but the car was at an angle heading for the curb. He swung the wheel, fingers gripping the leather cover. Paper and cigarette butts flew into the air as the wheels disturbed their resting place. He was in control again. Talk about a near-death experience! Dex thought. It was too much. He had to stop. He could feel vomit rising from the adrenaline surge he had just experienced. He drove a bit farther and pulled up at a lay-by.

He turned the engine off and turned to the girl. Her hand was white as it gripped the seat belt. The music blared out from the speakers in the back of the car, but he did not turn it off. It fuelled him. The girl turned to him, her face showing a mixture of shock and excitement. His hand slid on to her leg and worked upwards. Her hand fumbled for the release catch on her seat belt, then she slid out of the belt, the metal locking piece hitting the window with a thud as it flew back. They ravished each other in a surge of lust, avoiding the gear stick that stood between them.

Chapter Four

Family Reunion

Friday night had come with the setting sun. It had been a symbol too for drinking and speeding to Dex and his friends. The night people emerged in their best clothes, their perfumes and aftershaves smelling seductively, and their purses and wallets loaded with money for the night ahead.

He followed a group of clubbers to a well-known haunt of his where he had stalked with hunger many a time, its entrance bringing a strange comfort to him. He would find a hit here certainly. He paid and entered, scanning the club, and felt the eyes look him over. He read their minds but found nothing of interest. In fact he was not sure if he had started a new fashion with his red lenses, as a number of people now wore them in different shades and styles. He allowed himself a smile and went down among his followers.

He sensed around, using his mental 'feelers' to find the perfect one or two. Then he found it. His stomach churned as he saw a woman wearing shades like himself in the corner: a follower. He went over and asked her if she wanted a drink. He bought drinks and introduced himself. They talked for a while under the pounding music that boomed from the gigantic speakers, and soon they left – back to her place.

He sensed something different about her, a quality that

none of his other hits had ever had, but she had narcotics in her system. It was some new drug, he concluded; it was nothing he had sensed before. But still something disturbed him slightly: not a danger, exactly, but something mysterious.

They left the taxi which had brought them and entered her home, an old house which had been divided into flats. Her home was at the back, her kitchen overlooking a half-empty rubbish skip in the back garden. When she locked her front door, he could feel his fingernails begin the itch again, in anticipation of his nocturnal feed upon her. She invited him into her living room, which contained an illuminated fish tank glowing in the darkness. With the flick of a switch she revealed the rest of the room, furnished with expensive taste. Perhaps she worked in the decor or furnishing business, he wondered to himself. He was finding it difficult to pick her mind. She seemed as mysterious as the shaded glasses she still wore; she could have been a double of himself, in a way.

'Would you like a drink? Coffee? Tea?' she asked, adjusting the dial for the living-room spotlights, making them more subdued.

'Coffee would be fine,' he replied, making himself comfy on her stylish sofa.

'Milk? Sugar?'

'Neither, I drink it black.'

She could work for a fashion magazine, or something in that line of work, he thought. Her enigmatic aura was making his powers ineffective. He did not like the feeling of mystery; it made him uneasy.

A few minutes later she returned with two cups of coffee which she placed on two spider's-web-design coffee mats, before sitting down beside him.

'Drink,' she said in a sultry tone.

He knew this would be an easy hit. She was willing, and

he could spend all evening draining her of whatever narcotic lay dormant in her system... and enjoy it.

She crossed her legs, revealing white flesh while she sipped her coffee. The hunger rose in him like a disturbed beast; his fingers were tingling at the thought of action. Her presence next to him excited him, and he could feel the needles ready to extend. Easy now, easy! he said to himself. She leaned towards him, his face reflected in her lenses, her lips moist with coffee, her body poised to strike at him with lust, smooth hands sliding over his legs. He moved his mouth towards her slightly parted lips, almost touching; her lipstick was the colour of his lenses, her tongue slowly, erotically tracing her lips. Then they kissed. Lips bounded by desire, lust and addiction, violently burst with passions unknown to him. He was aroused in a way he had never known before, different from usual, something more than carnal. Never had kissing held so much for him before. Her arms embraced him tightly, then he slipped his arms around her waist, trapping her with his presence. The needles began to grow, exiting from under his nails, and he traced her spine with them underneath the black dress she wore. He poised himself in readiness, waiting to strike. Then he felt a sharp pain at the base of his spine.

He broke away in a rage of pain and confusion, pushing her from him, feeling some sharp object slide out of his back. He clutched her hand, trying in the subdued light to see the weapon she had used on him, but saw nothing – only a number of needles receding back under the finger-nails of her left hand. It took seconds to register the sight, but then his mind blanked out in disbelief at what he had just seen. It could not be.

'Who are you...?' he mumbled, in shock.

She sat silent, her eyes looking at his own needles going back.

'How can this be?' he demanded, now a little in control.

He found himself shaking, and got up to leave, trying to escape this madness.

'Come back! You cannot leave!' she cried out, following him and grabbing his arm. He turned to face her.

'How is this *possible*?'

They stood, unmoving, lost for words, their hearts beating in time. She removed her lenses revealing pale eyes, the pupils almost bleached. He gasped, then slowly removed his own to reveal the same.

★

In the local cemetery, Dex pulled up his jeans, casually flinging away the used condom; the dead already knew what they had been up to, anyway, he thought. It had been a good night. Some good speeding, almost death, and now the girl who lay at his side. The girl, lying half-naked on the grass, moaned his name, but he ignored her. She had been just another shag, that was all.

'Got to be off,' was his only reply.

'Wait on,' she moaned, pulling up her dress, which was stained with grass and spilt alcohol from the pub. 'Where are we going?'

'Have to get home,' he answered, feeling irritated by her presence now.

'Yours or mine?'

Shit! Dex thought, this one was going to be hard to get rid of.

★

Lou heard her mother go into the bathroom, doped up on Valium again. She waited until she was sure she was in the bath, then pulled out her black book of telephone numbers from the inside pocket of her denim jacket.

She sat on the stairs next to the telephone and looked through the black book until she found the name she wanted. She picked up the receiver and dialled. She counted the rings on the other end. She waited, but there was no reply. She put down the receiver and flicked through again, finding the other name. She dialled.

'Yep, Jimmy here. Who is it?'

'Jimmy, is Lou.'

'How's your head today?' he asked with laugh. It had been a hectic session, the night before.

'Banging a bit – the head shake all day.'

'I told you not to take that stuff. Looked cheap and nasty – pure head-bang inducing stuff. What can I do you for? I haven't got much time; I'm out tonight.'

'Who are you out with?'

'Ronny and the lads.'

'Oh yeah, I know them,' she answered. She more than just knew them; she had slept with nearly all of them.

'What's up, anyway?' he asked.

'Jimmy, have we ever…?'

'What?'

'Have we ever…?'

'Drunk together? Danced? What?'

She despaired, he always had to do this. He could be a right wanker sometimes, but he was still a mate.

'Have we ever screwed?' she finally put it, subtle as hell.

He was speechless. The other end of the line was silent.

'Jimmy? Are you there?'

'Yeah, I'm here. I was just taken back. It's the first time I've heard you use the word "screw", that's all. You normally use "fuck".'

'Have we. Have we ever "fucked" then?'

'I don't think so. Unless I've been pissed out of my head.'

'Thanks, I just had to know. See you for now.'

She put down the receiver before he said anything else. At least it wasn't him. That was one off the list. My life just seems to be just one long orgy, she thought. She couldn't remember faces sometimes when off her head, or when she felt herself penetrated by rubber in the early hours of the morning. When she was in a 'loved-up' state she just went with the flow; nothing held back her chemically-aroused mind and body on a night out. She flicked through the black book again... searching, hoping.

★

He and she now sat in silence, coffees going cold, the milk on the surface curdling, their minds thinking alike. They had the same thoughts, but one question still remained unknown to them – how had they lived without knowing somehow that they had a relation? Some psychic sense should have told them, but it had not. Two beings, rare creatures of the same kind, in the same town. He felt elated now after the shock revelation. He felt a dream come true, become reality. He was alone no more.

'Sister...' he said, more as a thought than a word.

She looked at her brother, her twin.

'Yes?'

He looked at her, studied her face, and saw a faint resemblance there – his mother's face from a photograph shown to him many years ago.

'Do you remember Mother?' he asked.

'Only from a photograph,' she replied, feeling an ache for the mother she never knew, 'which Dr Branag showed me.'

'He never told me I had a sister,' he said, remembering the baby who apparently died when he had been born. 'I have spent years dreaming, hoping for someone – a relation, a companion – but would never have believed...'

'I know how you feel. I felt the same way myself. Even though Dr Branag kept us apart, I knew I was not alone. At least he did make sure we did not go out into the world incapable of surviving,' she said, looking around her furnished flat.

'How do you afford it?'

'Rich boyfriends,' she said with a smile.

'Boyfriends? How do you have any kind of relationship, given the life you lead?'

'They think of me as some kind of eccentric, wearing shaded glasses all the time. If they're not rich, then they're addicts who I drain and dispose of.'

'You mean *kill*.'

'No. I do not drain them to death, only to the edge of death. I keep them for a while, use them and leave them,' she explained.

'I see,' he said in reply, relaxing back in her armchair and looking upwards at one of her spotlights.

'When is our birthday?' she asked.

'June, some time. I think we are Gemini.'

'The twins,' she commented, discovering something more about herself. 'Then you would be the elder by a few minutes.'

He remembered back to the nightmare birth, the doctors and the suited men looking down on them like it was some freak show. No one helped the mother. They were more interested in the birth of the ultimate junkies.

'They were waiting for years for us, waiting to see if addiction could be passed down the generations and what the results were,' she said quietly. 'We were bound to turn out—'

'Unnatural,' he interrupted.

She found the word painful to bear, but there was no other word.

'Yes,' she replied, after composing herself.

They were silent for a while. The mention of the person so close to them, the person who had brought them into this world, dragged up painful memories which they wished they had left in the past.

'Why is addiction such a terrible thing?' he asked.

'You mean, why did Mother continue with her injections even when we were growing inside her womb? Our whole family were addicts, or alcoholics. We were narcotic babies – the first and hopefully the last.'

Her hunger was beginning to eat away inside her. She needed a hit, and desperately. She could not survive the night without some narcotics inside her.

'You're hungry,' he said.

'Yes! The night is still young – we can still find a hit or two together, now that we've met each other.'

The thought felt beautiful to him: brother and sister, hunting in the night for hits, searching for victims. Being as one. Together at last.

Chapter Five

Student Demise

They hit the town, heading towards the university campus where a number of cheap watering holes flourished with student grant money. Scuffer's seemed ideal for their needs, an underground music bar which sometimes had aspiring musicians from around the country playing punk tunes. But tonight was dance night with a scruffy looking DJ mixing records together with enthusiasm, even though the clientele was more interested in the booze and joints they had. As the sound of wailing horns on one techno track boomed out from the speakers it was like a warning siren going off as he and she went down amongst the dancers with a hunting passion.

They looked around, scanning, searching, sensing for something powerful. Spliff smokers would not sort them out; they needed something stronger as the hunger ate away inside them. Then, near the toilets, the sound of breaking glass caught their attention. A girl lay on the floor, and her boyfriend went down to pick her up, apologising drowsily to the person whose drink had just been knocked over. The drowsiness of the couple appealed to him and her; it was the torpor of taking hard drugs: heroin.

They met up with the couple when they finally sat down and started a conversation with them on dealing drugs. He and she read their minds. The boy was Irish, and an ex-choirboy now turned junkie student, a V-sign to his staunch Protestant parents. The girl who had just fallen was from Newcastle and from a broken home, and only at college through some government scheme to get the unemployed back at work; the money they gave her went straight into the vein. The young couple needed a hit, as did he and she; it would be a marriage made in Heaven or Hell. With the offer of cheap heroin given to them on a silver platter – a lie, of course – the young couple followed him and her home, back to her flat, where they stumbled in. The couple's minds were empty of any thought but the promised hit.

Inside, they drank, and finally became involved in a foursome after the couple was allowed a small dose of their drug from her small private supply. Clothes were scattered on the floor as their bodies sweated; an eager anticipation arose in him and her, an anticipation the couple would not expect. The couple would not know real ecstasy until death came to claim them.

Three hours passed while he and she relaxed, drinking and talking of the past, present and future while their hits lay bound and gagged on the bed, moaning with the taste of ecstasy they had been given. But the best was yet to come.

'How are you feeling?' he asked her.

'Beautiful, just beautiful,' she purred, stretching out her arms in ecstasy.

'How can we get rid of them… the bodies?'

'The skip out the back. We can dress them, dump them in there and let it be taken away. Another two young people lost to the dangers of drug abuse.'

'You've thought of everything,' he replied. 'Have you done this before?'

'Once or twice, but I don't always kill them. I had one once who was covered in needle marks. I kept him for a week, feeding him occasionally, draining him bit by bit. It was a very pleasant experience – drugs on tap!'

He smiled at the thought, then said, 'Shall we?' he indicated their victims lying bound and gagged on the bed.

'We shall.'

'After you,' he said with courtesy.

She stood up and walked over to the boy and gazed down upon him, the bedroom spotlight illuminating his flesh, and then she felt her needles start to grow stiff in the approaching excitement. She licked her lips in anticipation.

'What a beautiful pair they make,' she commented.

Then something caught her eye. A golden crucifix on the boy's chest was attached to a chain round his neck. She wrapped it around one of her needles and examined it. Old habits die hard; always the choirboy, she thought. Looking at the needle marks on his arm and the religious icon on his chest, she said to herself, What would the vicar say?

Then they sunk in their needles, giving their victims pure ecstasy behind their gags. Then they blew their minds away.

The girl saw him remove his underwear and reveal a large hypodermic needle where his penis should have been, spraying out heroin solution over her body, then forcing the needle inside her, entering her in a chemical sex act that made her lose her remaining sanity. She was beyond screaming.

The boy looked up and saw her, dressed as a Roman centurion, driving needles through his hands and feet into a large wooden crucifix. He could feel the blood seeping down the contours of his face as a crown of hypodermics was pressed down on to his scalp – the King Junkie. Then she took a giant hypodermic and raised it up above his body and drove it down into his side like a spear. That was the last image he ever saw.

Chapter Six

Table for Two

Saturday came with the arrival of a truck to take away the skip that contained the hits from the night before. He left, after arranging to meet his sister for lunch in the city centre. He decided to walk home in the morning sun and prepare himself for the evening ahead, for she had planned a hit that made him thirst with hunger.

As he walked down the main road that led to his neighbourhood, he heard a car pull up at one of the houses, stereo blasting out and making people look out from their windows with disapproval. He turned his head towards the car, not seeing another that reversed out of the driveway he was just passing, the driver only noticing him at the last minute. A pain shot through his leg as the rear bumper hit him and he lost his balance, falling to the pavement.

He heard the car stop and the driver get out and help him to his feet, but then he realised that his eyes were burning with red-hot pain.

'My lenses!'

'They're here,' said the driver, picking them up and placing them in his hand.

He slipped them on and looked at his helper. She was a fortyish woman, two kids, part-time job – his powers were working well this morning.

'Thank you,' he replied, his voice a little strained.

'Are you sure you're okay?'

'A little dazed,' he replied.

'Come on in, I'll make you a drink.'

After moving the car back up the driveway and locking it, she led him into the house, sat him down and made him coffee. He could sense something about her – a slight possibility of a hit. She was a Valium taker. It would give him a mild boost, with no pain to her, only ecstatic pleasure.

'Perhaps I should ring for an ambulance,' she said, worrying.

'No,' he said abruptly. 'I shall be fine. You only jarred my leg a little. I'll be fine after a rest.'

'If you're sure…'

'I am. Thank you for your concern.'

She left the room and he looked at his hand; it trembled slightly. He could not remember the last time he had felt shaken. Maybe it was never.

His eye caught a picture on the mantelpiece, a family photo. Parents and children were huddled together against a winter background. One of the things he would never enjoy, even with his sister now. Or ever enjoyed in the past. The life of a loner could be painful sometimes.

'They're my kids,' said a voice behind him, his host.

He had realised that he was now holding the photo in his hands, having got up from his seat and picked it up subconsciously in thought.

'I'm sorry,' he said, putting the photo back.

She moved over to where he was standing and looked at the photo.

'What are their names?' he asked.

'Dexter and Louise.'

He looked at their smiling faces, red with the winter cold. They would be in their late teens now, he thought. While they were having their picture taken he was probably draining some poor addict dry. In a way he wished he was there, in the picture, feeling the closeness of the family, enjoying the winter together. But life threw you in different directions.

'And this is your husband?' he asked, pointing to the man with his arms around them all in the picture.

She was silent for a while, then spoke with pain in her voice, 'He *was* my husband.'

'I'm sorry.'

'My husband, John, died about fourteen years ago. I forget sometimes,' she mumbled, feeling a tear start to form in her right eye. 'It seems so long ago, now.'

'I am sorry, truly.'

He wanted to comfort her, make her trust in him. The Valium in her made him feel hunger, but the sensitive side of his nature, which had now been awakened, overpowered it and made him feel for this woman. She was a Valium taker, perhaps, to hide her personal pain. Sometimes drugs were not used merely for pleasure, but as painkillers too – both physically and emotionally.

As if some inner control had taken over, he took her head and rested it on his shoulder. She did not resist as her tears fell on to the material of his shirt and soaked into the fabric. He saw the whole thing in his mind – the car crash, the exploding glass, the blood. But the pain would not end there, never.

The closeness awakened his hunger. The physical presence of the woman with the Valium inside her, here with him, was too much a temptation. He tried to fight it, but the vampiric nature that he possessed overrode his struggle. He had to drain her. He felt his needles begin to stiffen and he slowly sank them into her. She winced for a second, then her tears seemed to stop as she looked into his face with an air of wonder. She started to feel dazed, and her muscles started to slacken as a pure joy entered her. She arched her back as he slid them in further, making her gasp with delight. A surge of pleasure channelled through her body, exciting her, stimulating her. His own body shuddered as the Valium entered his body, his needles sucking and draining her to emptiness.

She had never felt ecstasy like it. Even her husband, when he had been alive, had never given her such an orgasm. She felt weak at the knees and her muscles gave way totally until he was holding her upright. She could offer no resistance towards him, her will for the time being broken, her soul sold to the gift he was giving her.

When he had drained her completely, he laid her down on the sofa and felt her pulse – she was alive but in a state of utter exhaustion. He left her as she was and went out of the house. The Valium took away the pain in his leg, and he walked home healed and slightly invigorated.

Lou came home and found her mother on the sofa, asleep and with a look of contentment on her sleeping face. She looked down and turned away from her in disgust.

Valium and whisky, she said to herself.

She knew all about her mother's daytime habits. She only hoped that she would be still asleep when she went out to Zeppelins in the evening. At least she could get out of the house without another argument.

Dex was in two minds about Zeppelins. The prospect of willing girls hyped up and ready for anything (as Neil had put it) appealed to him, but the idea of having it off with some psyched-out druggie made him feel somewhat uneasy. She would be getting pleasure out of the drug she had taken earlier rather than anything he would be giving her.

He made a decision and went to Neil's house to buy a ticket, even though he needed a new wing mirror for his car and Neil still owed him forty quid.

★

He went home and locked the front door behind himself. He felt weary, the recent experience and the night before made him want to catch up on some sleep. He slumped down on his sofa and closed his eyes behind his lenses, and drifted off into sleep quickly and easily.

He was dreaming of her: the sister, the twin he never thought he had. But what he dreamt disturbed him; something about the images he saw made him uneasy. He could see her wandering around back alleyways and seedy pubs looking for men that she could lure back to her flat. But the final image woke him from the dream. It was a horrifying image of a young man lying face down in a bowl of speed while she straddled his back, forcing needles into his arms. She pumped him and made him ingest the drugs she had for him, then she drained him with her own needles with a look of sexual satisfaction on her face. But this was no nightmarish image. From this he knew that his sister not only drained drugs like himself to survive, but she actually enjoyed it, using her survival technique for her own pleasure. She was an addict herself, filling her victims with drugs then removing them with almost orgasmic pleasure. It was one addict living off another addict – with no remorse if the victims died in mid-draining. He had never seen himself as an addict, only a creature who must drain to survive; to him it was a noble act, not that of a perverse pleasure-seeker. It was true what they said about twins: one soul shared, but two entirely different personalities – opposites, almost... good and bad, the hunter and the hunted. But who between them was the hunter and who was the hunted?

He got up and washed himself, waking himself up and preparing to meet his sister for lunch. The dream still disturbed him, but he tried to put the thoughts away and not let them spoil the first time he and his sister had ever eaten together in each other's company.

They met each other in a stylish restaurant in town. He joined her at the table where she sat sipping mineral water. He ordered some lunch and watched her finish hers.

'Best line the stomach for tonight,' she said to him when the waiter departed with his order.

'Absolutely.'

When his lunch had arrived, they stared at each other trying to read each other's minds.

'Let's talk instead,' she suggested.

'Have you ever been in love?' he started, sipping onion soup from his spoon.

'Love? Never in my existence. I have never known what love is,' she replied.

'How about attraction?'

'Only once,' she said, fidgeting with her glass of mineral water.

'May I ask who?'

She seemed somewhat apprehensive about answering, but she assumed a relaxed air and answered.

'A man I once met in a bar. He was an urban poet – wrote about lower-class struggle, unemployment, petty crime, kids hooked on solvents and drugs... the usual gloom. But he was the only man I had met whom I could talk to and understand what he was saying, and in some way understand my own life in doing so. Although he seemed to think of me as some social outcast who hides behind shaded lenses to escape from some problem I have with life, he was so close to the truth.'

'He understood the pain and loneliness?'

'I suppose he did, yes.'

'Was he an addict?' he probed.

'No!' she said abruptly, 'he was not.'

She regained her calmness. I've touched a nerve there, he thought to himself.

'Then why do I sense your sadness?'

She said nothing, transmitting her thought outwards to him, seeing if he could pick them up; his probing made her feel uneasy and irritated.

'You have suffered a broken heart,' he concluded, looking deep into her hidden eyes. She stared back at him and put a thought directly into his mind.

'He was a... homosexual,' he said, catching her thought.

'Yes,' she said. 'He liked me as a friend, a companion almost, someone he thought was like himself in a way, someone he could talk to – not as an item of lust. At first I was a little broken up about it but then realised it would never have worked out if he did want me as a partner in a relationship. What if he did find me attractive, and I told him that I had to go out and drain a few druggies occasionally at weekends instead of visiting his parents or something? I was created to be alone – as you were.'

Her story awakened the pain in his own body, the savage anger of the social outcast wanting to be recognised and find normal life, love and friendship. But he did have a love in his life now, a woman, too: his twin sister.

After eating they left and walked towards the club where they would be going that night, eyeing the place over, looking for somewhere to get in without having to pay by using the normal entrance and exit.

'What is this place called?' he asked, checking the door at the back of the building.

'Zeppelins. They have raves here sometimes. They're having one tonight,' she explained.

'Rave night. No alcohol. Just water.'

'And plenty of drugs. They have security checking but they sell their own supply inside. A nice little sideline business,' she remarked.

'And I bet there will be a lot of chemically enhanced people tonight.'

'It will be Heaven: a massive orgy of narcotics, taking the

drugs out of people in minor doses to make the night last longer and not to overdose ourselves,' she said with a smile.

He had an image in his head now of his sister going round with a hypodermic and purposefully injecting people then draining them later on in the night, all through the night.

'What are you thinking?' she asked, looking for the answer in his mind.

He looked at her and let her read his mind.

'You think I find draining them sexy and orgasmic. Don't tell me you don't find it pleasurable – the draining and excreting our fluids and the narcotic mixing together like sexual juices in intercourse!'

'I find it pleasurable. But it disgusts me too,' he replied.

'Disgusts you? What are you, some kind of monk?' she laughed. 'It seems I am the twin who is able to live my life not as some lonely crusader with a rage against society and oneself. I am a hunter, a pleasure-seeker, using other people's lives to make mine last longer, and have fun doing it.'

'What does that make me then? The hunted?'

She looked at him quizzically.

'Why do you say that?' she asked.

'I am the opposite. I live the life of a hunted man, trying to live each day as it comes, fearing the time when it will end, hunted and isolated by the world around me. I drain people out of rage and for survival rather than pleasure.'

'Perhaps,' she replied, 'you need to live a little. I think tonight should cure that.'

He nodded wearily. She was right, his entire life had been like that of a hunted man, fearful of the one day when the world would find him out and persecute him, his anger directed inwards in fear rather than out against it.

'Do you think you can open the door?'

He looked down at the lock he had been inspecting and

turned to her. 'Should be easy. I have a lock-picking set at home. Should prove no problem.'

They walked away, making their way back home and talked.

'Better wear something light; these places can get very hot,' he said to her as they strolled down one of the city's main roads. Then something made him contort his face in disgust, his nose wrinkle and his skin crawl.

She could feel it too – a sickening smell and sensation coming from somewhere, making them want to vomit.

'What is it?' she demanded.

He looked around for what was exuding the smell, then he saw it. A half-bottle of beer discarded by some careless drinker under a bush.

'Alcohol!' she said in disgust.

They vacated the area quickly and when they were out of the bottle's range they let out a sigh of relief and gasped in the more appetising smell of exhaust fumes.

'Good,' he said.

'Have you ever taken any alcohol?' she asked, breathing in lungfuls of polluted air.

'Never, it has always made me feel sick, even the smell of it.'

'I did once, it almost killed me. I suppose it was stupid of me really, but I wanted to know what was happening in the world around me, so I gave it a try.'

'What happened?'

'I was in bed for a week. My body was weak, my skin in a terrible condition. I really thought I was going to die. I only had a drop on my tongue, and it almost killed me.'

'Not an experience I would like to go through,' he said.

'I suppose we would be able to sense if someone had been drinking alcohol tonight if they were at Zeppelins, wouldn't we?' she asked.

'I would have thought so.'

They walked on, totally recovered from their bad experience.

'Father died from alcohol,' she said.

He did not reply. This was the chemical addiction that people still treated as harmless. Their father had become addicted to it and now his children had become the victims of it. It was the only drug that would kill them. And it was legal too.

Chapter Seven

Injecting Erotica

He went back to his flat and showered, slipped on a pair of dark jeans ands pulled out a thin T-shirt and left the flat to meet her at her home. When he arrived she was in the shower, so he let himself in with the spare key she had given him and made himself a cool drink. It was a warm evening which would get warmer in the club they were visiting. He felt the hunger stir but he took his mind off it.

She came out of the shower and dried, then slipped into a tight dress with press studs up the back.

'Could you help me?' she asked.

He got up and walked up behind her and started to connect the studs up her back, following her spine slowly, feeling the closeness between them.

'My dress is not straight.'

He smoothed it down her body, feeling something he had never felt before emerge from within him: a different hunger. When his hand smoothed over one of her breasts he knew it was wrong, feeling this way towards his sister.

'It is not wrong,' she whispered to him, pressing his hand more firmly against her breast. 'We are not restricted by normal human relationships.'

He could feel the heaving of her breast, the rhythm of it like he was listening to some music, such beautiful music. Her hand went behind her to smooth his thigh, and worked upwards towards his crotch, where she cupped him with her palm, fingernails testing the material of his jeans. His other hand slid across her flat stomach and slid over her crotch, resting there.

A spark ignited between their minds, a physical attraction growing between them. Slowly he felt his penis begin to harden to her touch, and she felt her vagina grow moist at his pressure.

She moved her fingernails away from his crotch as she felt her needles begin to grow, and the urge to plunge them into him and exchange fluids with him fired her imagination. She looked down to see his needles already erect and stroking her breast.

He kissed her neck, and the wetness of his lips on her sensitive skin made her slide her needles into him, puncturing the material of his shirt and going into the flesh and muscles of his stomach. He gasped with pleasure and located an entry point for his own needles. As they slid in effortlessly she emitted a moan from her lips. Their fluids mixed, ecstasy soared through their bodies, their veins, their minds, their senses buzzing with a new-found pleasure.

They were united, physically, spiritually and emotionally.

Chapter Eight

Family Atomic

Dex came in again after parking his car and found his mother asleep on the sofa, mumbling to herself. She was starting to wake and her eyes rolled in the throes of wakening.

'Where are you…?' she drawled.

Dex looked down in bemusement.

'I'm here, Mum. It's Dex.'

Her eyes looked at his dozily, almost smiling.

'Where is he?' she said, relaxed and calm for once, talking in a whisper.

'Who, Mum? Who?' he said, stroking her hair, trying to understand.

'The man,' she muttered, falling back into sleep again.

'Man? What man?' Dex asked, gently shaking her back to wakefulness.

'The one whom I knocked down…'

Knocked down? thought Dex. She must be imagining it, dreaming. He looked around to see if there was any trace of this man, but only a single coffee cup lay half-empty on the table. It was not unusual for his mother to act like this; she often talked in her sleep after a whisky and Valium fix.

'There's no one here, Mum.'

'He was here…'

She slipped back into sleep and Dex went upstairs in defeat. He was going to have a shower and get ready to go out when he realised that Lou was in the bathroom already.

Typical, he said to himself and went into his bedroom. There, he slipped in a CD and lay on the bed and thought about what to wear for the coming night. He looked out and saw the sun beginning to set.

Lou dried off her hair with the towel and went into the bedroom, hearing Dex's own bedroom door open and him mutter, 'About time!'

'Piss off,' she replied and plugged in her hairdryer, blasting her damp hair with hot air. While combing and drying she thought about what to wear for the night. She was meeting Justine at her house, then off to a couple of cheap clubs first, and then they'd hit Zeppelins and have the time of their lives – music pounding their senses, chemicals to get them high, and lads, lads, lads…

When her hair was dry enough to comb she looked through her bulging wardrobe and her expanding collection of clothes. Now came the worst part – the decision. She finally plumped for red hot pants and a red Lycra top, and with them flat-heeled shoes. Through experience she had discovered that it was dangerous to dance wildly in high-heeled shoes, so flat shoes were a must for any dance club.

When she was ready she found her ticket and went downstairs.

Dex came out of the shower and dried himself off, walking into his bedroom and looking down on his accessories for the night ahead. He chose a skinny T-shirt, black jeans and his recently bought fashionable trainers – and the most important items of all – condoms.

He had a feeling this was going to be a strange night: exhilarating but different; a totally new experience. Perhaps something he could get a buzz out of. He dressed and went downstairs to get a quick snack. Then he would have a few beers at the pub where he was due to meet the college bunch before going on to Zeppelins.

Lou heard Dex come down and braced herself for some remark to fall from his lips about her choice of evening wear.

'Where do you think you're going?'

She could not believe he had said that.

'Out! Where do you think dressed like this?' she replied.

'I thought you were under house arrest after last Thursday.'

She was and she was hoping that he wouldn't wake Mum. If that happened, her night out would be finished before it had begun.

'So what?' she replied in a pissed-off tone. 'Who do you think you are, my dad?'

Dex's face dropped and then she realised she had touched on a nerve there.

'What?' he asked, hardly believing his ears.

She wanted to go, but she knew that Dex would not leave it at that.

'You've got a fucking nerve!' he cried, closing the kitchen door and hopefully blocking out any noise that might wake Mum.

'Here we fucking go again! The older brother shit!'

'You're right! Ever since Dad died I've had to hold this family together.'

'This again!' she said with despair. 'You always think you're right, don't you? The apple of Mum's eyes, the proud son. But you're not. By the time you're thirty you'll be thinking of the good old days of shagging and getting pissed up and speeding around and wishing that you'd never done it, because you'll be overweight with some tart with a kid she says is yours and picking up your dole money every two weeks because you failed at college!'

'You fucking little—!' he screamed, raising a fist.

'Go on, then! Are you going to hit me? Eh?'

He took a step back and tried to calm down. But he

couldn't, he was too fired up.

'You're nothing, Dex. You're reckless; you force your own opinions on to other people. You think you're right all the time, and if no one agrees with you, you hate them. You've nothing to live for, no plans, no dreams. You don't think about anyone but yourself!'

He tried to close his ears but he couldn't. He felt trapped and exposed, as if his sister had just opened him up with a scalpel and exposed his life and future to the whole world. Images of his father plagued his mind.

'You're like Dad was! Getting drunk and driving at stupid speeds!'

Dad... he could see the car, the exploding glass, the blood. Seeing his dad die while he was strapped into the back seat.

'You're reckless, just like Dad was!'

He couldn't block out the words. They cut his mind like a razor, the truth ringing out at him.

'*Shut it*! How would you know? You weren't even there! I saw it all! I saw him die! *I saw Dad die!*'

She looked at him and said nothing. She saw the remembrance in his face, in his eyes; perhaps she had pushed this too far. But it was the truth and it needed pushing. Dad had always been reckless – in youth and in fatherhood.

'He was speeding, Dex. Speeding to get home. Not giving a fuck about you or Mum. He didn't even bother about strapping you into the back of the car properly. You were lucky! And what for? A fucking football match on the telly! Can you believe that? A *football* match! He risked yours and Mum's life that night. Perhaps even mine, if I'd have been there; but I was at Aunt Ellen's. Face it, Dex, he was no idol figure for anyone, not even you, even though you did idolise him and still do! If you can't accept it then one day you'll have to, when you end up like him – and what for? Because you don't give a shit about anyone but yourself! What kind of behaviour is that, eh?'

She left, slamming the door behind her and leaving Dex to consider what she had just said and maybe find some truth there.

The fresh air hit Lou as she stormed out of the house, calming her down as she made her way to Justine's house. Her head seethed with anger. She felt better for having the argument, and letting all that repressed anger come out. Maybe she had gone too far about Dad and his influence on Dex; but he had to be told, he had to know. He was his father's son, totally – too much like Dad. She had only vague memories of him. She was barely four when he had died. And she'd had no father for the rest of her life, just a mother who could only get by in life with Valium and whisky, and a brother who lived in Dad's reckless shadow. What a family, she thought. Family atomic...

Dex swept up the fragments of broken plates on the kitchen floor and rubbed his head as if he was trying to rub it clean of confusion and anger. At least the anger in him had come out on the crockery and not Lou. Hitting her would have made him feel much worse, perhaps make him feel more like Dad. The thought hurt but Lou had been right; painfully right. It was hard to admit, and admittance that he was following in his dad's footsteps disturbed him. Dad had never hit anyone, but the anger had always been there, below the surface, ready to explode. Did he have the same anger in him too?

He went in to see if Mum was now awake after the explosion of feelings and emotion, and the broken plates. She was still asleep. Dreaming of her man, probably. Dreaming of a replacement for Dad. He left locking the door behind him and leaving his mother to her dreams and hopes.

★

'Ready?' Lou called up the stairs at Justine's house.

'Just a minute,' answered Justine, slipping on her boots as Lou waited downstairs.

She came down and looked Lou over sensing something different about her.

'Something up?' she asked putting on her denim jacket.

'Nothing. I just had a big row with Dex.'

'Playing the parent again?'

'Don't mention anything about parents to me again. I'm well pissed off with them at the moment.'

'All right then. Are we off?'

'Yeah. It better be a good night. I need some fun right now otherwise I'll just end up whacking someone.'

They left Justine's house and made their way into town, but the row with Dex still hung over Lou like a black cloud.

'I can't cope with it any more. If it isn't Mum it's Dex. They're always getting at me. Everything I do is wrong, every decision is a problem, but they have more problems than I do! In fact I'm the only emotionally adjusted person in my family. Mum lives on whisky and Valium, Dex's mission in life is to endlessly shag girls and speed around, and Dad... well look at him now! He's dead – and why? Because of some stupid fucking football match!'

Lou couldn't help it; there was nothing she could do. The tears streamed down her face. She had lost control of all her emotions now, and they lay in tatters.

'What is it? What's the matter?' asked Justine, taking Lou in her arms and hugging her. Lou was silent for a while, then pulled away from her friend's embrace, and looked at her with tear-stained eyes.

'I'm pregnant.'

Justine looked at her, not believing what she had just heard.

'How... Whose is it?'

'I don't know. I can't think whose it could be.'

'You must have an idea. Tony? Jimmy?'

'I don't fucking know! It could be anyone.'

'Are you sure? It could be a phantom one.'

'I've been to the doctors. I am. I'm scared. Shit-scared, Jus. What am I going to do? Shit, I was only going on at Dex earlier about how he'll end up with some lass with a kid and waste his life, and look at me! I'm the lass with the kid who doesn't know who the dad is. I'm just going to be another single mother.'

'Abort it.'

Lou looked at Justine with confusion.

'I don't know, Jus. I really don't know,' she said, wiping her eyes of drying tears. 'I don't know really what to do.'

She stood for a while, calming herself.

'Come on. It doesn't matter for now. We're out to get away from all this stuff and have a good time.'

'It *does* matter though, Jus. It's my life, my family. My fucked-up life and family. But I'm not going to turn out like them, I'm not going to become just another statistic. No way! I need a fucking drink!'

They made their way to the nearest pub, even though they were under age.

Chapter Nine

Tablets and Needles

He and she now released themselves from their embrace and went out into the night refreshed and stimulated. Their hunger was even more ravenous now, the exchange of fluids giving them a bigger desire to drain narcotics. They could smell the scent of a new experience, a new hit. After that they would have to move city, even move country. The papers had printed a story about a Canadian executive dying from some chemical drug in his flat. It would not take long for other past cases to be linked with the latest. Things were hotting up. They would have to evade capture or be experimented on in some government lab and treated as freaks, their money taken away and whatever identities they had assumed in their lives buried away like they had never existed.

Tonight would be their leaving party of sorts. Europe looked promising: France; Holland – especially with its lax drug laws; Germany, in the east, where democracy had created a whole new drug empire for Western dealers.

'I'll miss the English junkies, you know,' she said with a touch of sarcasm.

'But think of the European junkies, think of them, cultured and sophisticated, they won't know what's hit them,' he replied with optimism. 'Come on! We have a rave to hit.'

Dex went through the pub doors to a welcome from his college friends and his final acceptance on the rave scene, something that he had always been apprehensive about since they had first known him.

'What's up?' asked Neil, noticing Dex's brooding appearance.

'Nothing, I just feel a bit shit at the moment. Let's just say you can never forget the past,' he explained. It was not exactly right, but it was the closest to an explanation he could think of.

'Never mind, have a pint. It's my round.'

That brightened Dex's spirits up – Neil buying a round. Wonders never ceased.

'What will you have?'

Dex gave him a weary look, the weary look of a man growing bored with his empty existence and behaviour. Lou had been right.

'The strongest thing in the pub.'

Lou and Justine had met up with the boy dressed in designer clothes in a regular haunt of theirs, a small club where they often started a night out.

'I've got the money,' Justine said to the boy, who only in his teens.

'Show me the money,' he demanded.

Lou could feel the eyes of the dealer's greasy-looking companion look her over. She felt uneasy and slightly giddy after the whiskies they had managed to get served in the pub. His leers made her want to smack him one, but the spark of violence just wasn't there. It had been in the kitchen, but not now. This was a time for fun. She ignored him.

'I've upped the price,' the dealer said.

'By how much?' Justine asked.

'Well, you haven't got enough there,' he said, looking at the note in Justine's hand.

'I can't afford more.'

'Well then, I suppose you could let Tone here have your mate for the night. Is it a deal?'

'Fuck off!' she replied.

'Only an idea,' said the dealer and smirked.

Lou and Justine waited there, hoping for him to drop the price to what it had been when they had last bought from him. He smiled with cigarette-stained teeth.

'Okay, you can have them at the previous price,' he said, closing the deal and reaching into the inside pocket of his jacket.

Lou looked at the tablets he held in his palm and could make out small smiling faces imprinted on them.

'Have a good night, ladies,' he said, as they took the tablets and gave him the money.

He and she watched a couple of girls in the corner of the club they were in, apparently haggling with two designer-clothed youths.

'Looks like someone is going to have a good time to-night,' she commented, leaning against him, her back against his chest.

They chose the club to get themselves set up for the rave later, and watched all the young people get into the mood of the night, dancing and swigging from their bottles of 'youth drinks'. Both of them still felt the eroticism and exhilaration of their recent encounter. Their mixed fluids buzzed around their veins, agitated. He could feel his fingernails itch again, and the urge to plunge his needles into her once again. With one hand he felt her body and she purred, almost catlike, at his touch. She started to rub his arm with her growing needles.

She could feel the music from the club's speakers have a subliminal effect on her mind and emotions and the feeling of her needles growing again turned her on. Talk about brotherly and sisterly love, she thought; it was practically incest. She gave a slight pant as she felt his needles enter her once again.

★

Dex came back from the pub's toilet to find all his mates were laughing at him – behind his back, or so it seemed. He was suspicious.

'What's so funny?' he asked with seriousness in his voice.

'Nothing,' said one of his fellow students, Isabelle. 'Liven up, Dex. We're supposed to be having fun.'

And with that she gave him a massive French kiss to cheer him up. It did. He had always fancied her since the first time they had met in the lunchtime pub across the road from the college… Things were looking up for the evening. He might even get off with her at the end of the night – he hoped. If he did he would be the happiest lad alive.

★

Lou took hers first, then Justine. They always took it in turns. Like a ritual. But they could never be sure if it was dodgy or not. This one seemed okay in there, but the gamble was not over yet, there was still a chance for something to go wrong but they had acquired a sixth sense now about buying and taking the drug. There were no warning bells this time.

'Are you ready for the night of your life?' shouted

Justine over the blasting music, her head bobbing to it.

'You bet I am!' replied Lou, her row with Dex now a faded memory.

'Look at them two over there. Weird or what?' Justine said laughing.

Lou looked over to where Justine was pointing, to see a couple in shaded lenses embracing each and in the throes of ecstasy, so it seemed. No clothes were undone or anything.

'Weird,' she replied.

He felt sensational. She had slipped in her own needles now and was secreting her own fluid into him again. He felt himself sweat and body perspire in writhing ecstasy as she ground her body against his, deeper and harder. Safe sex, he thought. Sharing needles can cause HIV: not in this case, she thought. Her needles, the music and the strobe lighting sent him to a seventh heaven and beyond. This was a new experience. This was the sex life he had always wanted. Now he had it.

They both moaned, trapped in a net of ecstasy and strobe lighting.

Chapter Ten

Bad Ecstasy

Dex and his mates had now left the pub and were making their way towards Zeppelins. Neil had said that getting there early was best as the queues could be long, even if you had tickets. When they arrived they saw the queue; not long but enough to keep them waiting a while.

'You'll love it,' Neil told him. 'This is *the* place to be.'

'Whatever, whatever,' Dex replied feeling lost without his car.

But Neil was right. As Dex flicked his dagger earring in irritation at the wait, the queue was moved forward bit by bit by the flak-jacketed bouncers asking for ID and searching randomly for concealed drugs, their radios buzzing with distant voices and interference. Dex wanted to be in there, feeling the surge of energy and female bodies dancing to the beat. He was right, Dex thought. I will love it. He couldn't stop eyeing up the girls in front of him, even though he had his sights on Isabelle. But what the hell, he was a reckless bastard anyway.

With that thought he dug his hands into his pockets and moved forward with the rest of the soon-to-be ravers.

As Dex flicked his earring in irritation, he and she, now out of their ecstatic embrace, knocked out a bouncer who was round the back of the rave club making sure no one was trying to get in illegally. But they were. His radio crackled on the floor as he slipped out his lock-picking set and set to work on the door.

When he had done the task he opened the door slowly, and let them peer into the doorway as if gazing into the entrance of another world. The music from inside thudded against the whole building, shaking the glass in the windows. The boom of music beckoned them, enticing them inside.

Oh, rave new world... she said to herself as she took a step through the doorway. He followed her, but into what? Was this to be a narcotic Heaven? Or would it be a narcotic Hell?

Lou and Justine got into Zeppelins just ahead of Dex and his friends, finding themselves in an arena of pounding bass, energetic flesh and blinding strobes. Banners with huge 'Z's imprinted on them hung from the ceiling and the atmosphere was brimming with energy. They wove their way through the people to get to the bar where they sold ice-cold bottles of water. Their thirst was in need of quenching now after the wait outside and they knew that a lot of water would pass their lips through the night and early hours of the morning, the fear of dehydration hung over everyone in the club.

'I needed that,' Lou said, after gulping down a mouthful of water from her plastic bottle.

'Yeah, I'm sweating already,' replied Justine, shouting into Lou's ear. The stifling atmosphere of body heat and sweat was affecting her already.

After refreshing themselves they moved off into the heart of the club.

Dex and his friends finally got in through the doors.

'*No lager!*'

Dex could hardly hear Neil under the music; Neil was explaining to him that alcohol was not served on the premises. That was a let-down, Dex thought to himself. But when Neil put an ice-cold bottle of water in his hand, its effect in the heat of the club cooled him down considerably. That made him a little happier. But the sight of young girls whose bodies moved intoxicatingly to the music like some ritual dance, exuding a sexuality that hypnotised him entirely – now that made him happier more.

This was Heaven.

He and she entered a group of people, the startling strobes subdued beneath their lenses, their senses alive with the scent of chemicals taken by the young hedonists around them.

She moved towards a young man in a yellow T-shirt whose sweat stains stood out under his armpit through her lenses. He exuded the Ecstasy aroma and she licked her lips in anticipation. She moved up close to him and slid in her needles as he began to kiss her neck like a maniac and grind his body against hers. A different 'ecstasy' flowed now into him as she felt him push his erection against her, the chemical he had taken flowing through her, draining him while he was occupied with her body. She withdrew her needles before the 'kiss of death' set in, felt him ejaculate and pushed him away from her, her victim staggering backwards, a damp stain of ejaculation marking the crotch of his jeans, and his mind and emotions in turmoil.

He made his way through the dancers picking his first victim. He was about to hypnotise her with his mental powers when something distracted him. He turned and saw her. It was not something she had taken that made him turn to her and change his victim. Something else had caught his attention. Her face – it was familiar. It was a face he had seen somewhere before, but now she had grown older. He thought back through his past but no bells rang in his brain. He was sure he'd seen her image recently – very recently.

Valium, he said to himself.

It was the Valium taker's daughter, he was sure. Older

now, in her teens. And a drug taker too – he could sense that now. Like mother, like daughter, he thought to himself, but for different reasons: one for pain and one for pleasure. In his lifetime he had never had two people from the same family before, and on the same day too. This was a bizarre coincidence, a fluke. Perhaps it was fate. He thought about leaving her, feeling unsure about the chance meeting, but he could not help the hunger raging inside him.

He moved towards her, his appetite whetted.

Lou was lost. Justine was beside her a moment ago but had now vanished in the crowd. She didn't feel well, there was something wrong with this tablet. She should have been feeling great, but something made her fear. She had heard of dealers mixing Ecstasy with other drugs, and that was what made her afraid. If it had been mixed, then what with?

She could feel the drug in her brain and she felt alone amongst all these people who crowded around her seemingly. She could feel masculine hands touch her body as people crushed themselves against her, their sexual appetites hungering for her young nubile body, like a sacrificial virgin. Hands pawed her into a corner, male and female fingers stroking and caressing her, clawing and molesting, their sexuality crossed and mixed... there were no taboos here, only pleasure on a high plane of hedonism.

Then a hand came from out of nowhere, grabbed her arm and pulled her away from her molesters and took her into an alcove in the club.

'Are you okay?' her saviour's voice whispered into her mind.

She nodded and saw the strobe lighting reflect surreally in the dark crimson of his lenses. It looked like the weird bloke in the club they had been before, she thought. It was a dead ringer, for sure.

His fingers brushed her hair gently and one hand slid

behind her back. His touch excited her and she let her lips open at the feel of the moist touch of his own lips on her flesh. Whoever he was, weird or not, she didn't mind at that moment, as there was something about him she had never felt before in any other male she had been with before. He was older, for sure, but age also meant experience.

She felt a sharp pain in her neck, then a warm glow seeped slowly down her neck into her body. A building of ecstasy was making her weaker and weaker so that she wanted to slip to the floor. It made her giggle, and slightly giddy, like the effects of some happy drug, but this sensation was something else. It came from him…

She let the sensation take its effect on her and fell into his embrace.

Dex had seen a woman and felt a sudden attraction. She stood by the wall and the lights reflected off her lenses like a light show of her own. As he moved towards her he knew something was not right, an alien sensation buzzed in his head.

'What's up?' asked Neil over the music.

'I don't know,' he replied.

'It can't be the drink!' Neil said, laughing.

A feeling of lift and a slight rush to his head entered his body, and suddenly he felt relaxed and also invigorated.

'You bastard!' Dex cried at him. 'You've slipped something into my drink!'

Neil laughed again and escaped into the crowd of dancers before Dex could recover from the realisation. Dex knew Neil had loaded his drink. In the pub earlier when he came out of the toilets, he saw them all laughing. It must have been then. Even Isabelle had been in on it. Fuck her and the rest of them! he thought, anger raging in him.

His mind reeled as he tried to find Neil in the crowd, but what anger he had inside him now slowly diminished as another feeling slowly took over him: stimulation. He felt his sexuality begin to roar into life again. He felt like a feline predator stalking its victim; the animal side of him was unleashed and his sexual urge now became uncontrollable.

He saw her again, against the wall by herself, scanning the dancers, or so it seemed. His vision seemed distorted now and other colours clouded his eyes. But she was still there as everything around her blurred into insignificance. Then a shattering vision blew his mind as he watched her. All around her flames danced in oranges, yellows and reds, and she herself, in tight red leather, crouched down with one red-gloved hand extended, her finger seductively beckoning him towards her. This was not Heaven. She was no angel. She was drawing him down into Hell, a hell in which she existed, and himself maybe. It was an offer he could not refuse. He was reckless and had always known it deep down. Lou had been right too. But this woman was pure recklessness, and he loved her for it.

He rubbed his eyes to clear them of the vision he had seen, and looked for her near the wall... she had gone. He went into the crowd determined to find her. Then he caught sight of the reflection of the strobe lights on her lenses and saw her with some man, embracing him. In his mind this man was nothing compared to himself; he knew what kind of woman she was. They were alike and they would both burn in Hell, wrapped together sexually until they were but ashes.

He took hold of her shoulder and pulled her away from the man she was with, catching sight of her fingers as they seemed to slide out of the man. She looked surprised at first but then a wicked grin came across her face. Her fingers looked like needles, he thought to himself. Jesus, it must be the drug Neil had slipped him! The vision, and now this. She drew up to him, her lips parting to him, beckoning him to slip in his tongue into her waiting mouth.

He accepted the invitation.

She felt a hand grab her shoulder and turn her round. The remnants of the acid she had just drained from the man she was with flowed through her veins and mind, and now the shock of being manhandled behind by some unknown assailant put her off; her senses were shaken out of place and control.

She looked into the face of the assailant and saw something there, something that pleased her. He was on something. She admired his gold earring with the small dagger that dangled from it and the golden stubble that covered his head. Her needles slipped out of her previous victim, who looked at her, dazed, and slid them behind this newcomer's back. Fingering his skinny T-shirt, she licked her lips with the tip of her tongue and moved closer to him, feeling his lips clamp passionately to hers, his tongue working away inside her mouth. Yet something niggled at the back of her mind. Something was not right. But she was caught up in the exhilaration she felt in the environment and the boy she was with to take any notice of any apprehensions she felt. She let her needles slide in and extract the chemical from him.

The slight worry she had just felt pounded through her brain now. A flash of imagery struck her mind, a vision of empty pint mugs and whisky glasses littering a bar. This was a bad hit. Something was very wrong. As the alcohol from Dex's bloodstream entered her, she let out a piercing scream.

Across the room, the scream seared through his mind, a jet of flame activating his senses. In a reflex action he pushed the girl away and turned to see where the scream had come from. He knew it was her. And she was in trouble. He fought his way through the dancers, his needles still stiffly extended and dangerous and came across the young man who she was with. She was on her knees, her back arched in crippling agony, her mouth wide open emitting the scream he had just heard. The young man she was with was trying to remove her needles from himself. He moved forward with violence and thrust his own needles savagely into the youth's chest, thoughts flicking through his mind. What had this youth done to her? The youth fought like a madman against him and her now, the two sets of needles lodged deeply into his anatomy. In the struggle they ended up sprawled across the dance floor, the ravers oblivious to what was going on next to them.

His hallucinogen entered Dex's system, but what he drained out from Dex was not a narcotic he was accustomed to. He felt the effect of it enter him and his skin began to crawl, the poison decaying his veins until he pulled away from the youth in a fit of convulsions. He fell next to her in throes of physical torment, their bodies reacting to the alien toxin that now destroyed them. Dex lay there, his mind whirling at the event, feeling the effects of the fluids they had injected into him seep slowly into his mind like a subliminal poison.

Chapter Eleven

Abortive Thoughts

Lou staggered against the wall, her body tingling with some strange sensation, her legs only just supporting her, her sexual juices flowing. But it was a scream that brought her to her senses now: a scream like no human scream, piercing and animalistic. Her eyes looked around her, her vision was hazy; she was seeing people being pushed aside by the man she had been with only moments ago. Her head thumped like a bad hangover and she started to see strange things in front of her. She could see Dex. Her brother – here at Zeppelins! It made no sense to her. Why would he be here? But why he was here was nothing compared to what she saw near him.

Two people, one of them the man she had just been with, were on the floor; the other was a woman who looked like the one her companion had been with in the previous club and they were both having a fit of some kind. This was too much, she thought to herself, making her way over to her brother who now stared at the couple in a trance-like state. What she saw next defied credibility. Fountains of blood began to spray from the couples veins on to Dex and anyone around them, soaking into clothes and the skin. This was all weird; the tablet she had taken must have been mixed with something else – acid or something; who knows? This was scary…

Then her body began to shiver as if an ice-cold draught

had just blown through the club. Her skin froze and went into goose pimples as she collapsed to the ground, hugging herself to keep warm as her body temperature began to drop rapidly. She could feel hands grabbing her arms and legs and moving her across the floor. Then her vision blurred to nothingness; no images could be seen. But a smell wafted to her nose, a clinical antiseptic smell of a hospital. She felt a tightness strain against her ankles and wrists. She was tied down spreadeagled on what seemed like a bed. A hand slapped her face, a hand wearing what felt like surgical gloves.

'*Wake up!*'

Her vision began to come back and she saw a face glaring down at her.

'Are you awake?'

She nodded and took in her surroundings. It was some surgery of some sort, bloodstained and unclean like some illegal backstreet clinic. She noticed she was wearing a surgical gown. A table of instruments lay by her side containing an array of menacing clinical instruments.

'What are you doing?' she asked.

Music blared from behind a plastic door, almost as if the club was in the same building.

'We're going to take your baby,' the surgeon said.

'What do you mean?'

The surgeon stared deep into her eyes and spoke through thin lips.

'The world is overpopulated, Lou. We don't need any more unwanted pregnancies in this country.'

He turned to a machine in the corner. It rested on a trolley and he wheeled it over to where her feet were restrained.

'We do not need any more useless flesh to bleed the economy dry, you slut! Use protection in future! I'm sick of all you careless teens!'

He switched on the machine and showed it to her. It had a long metal arm with a claw attached.

'You know where that's going, don't you?' he said, grinning through bad teeth.

She felt her vaginal muscles contract in fear at the thought. He couldn't! She fought against her restraints in vain.

'It's going all the way up, Lou, all the way up till I've got that little fucker in your womb. Then I'll rip it out!'

'*No*! *You bastard*!' she shouted, wrists rubbing agonisingly against her bonds. 'Get the fuck away from me!'

He picked up the machine and moved the clawed end up her gown and in between her legs.

'Get that fucking thing away from me!' she cried, spitting anger at him. The music from behind the plastic door increased so that it deafened her ears.

He lost his temper and punched her angrily in the mouth. Then he said, 'Shut it, you annoying bitch! I've got work to do!'

Her head banged against the hardness of the bed and she felt dazed, losing consciousness for a while. She felt the claw enter her and work its way upwards into her. She felt no pain. Only a wrenching feeling deep inside her as the claw clamped on the living foetus inside her. She screamed, not in pain, but in realisation that she was about to lose something that was hers, something that was living inside her, growing with her help, something that was part of her. She kicked wildly against the bonds, the music getting louder and louder. Lights were now starting to flicker through gaps in the plastic door, illuminating her and the surgeon in a bizarre light show.

And then there was a wailing sound. The surgeon laughed as he pulled free what had been inside her, a blood-covered creature that was the beginning of the human being. It had a mouth and it wailed like a newborn baby.

'Gotcha!' sneered the surgeon, dropping the foetus on the trolley.

'*Get off my fucking baby, you bastard!*'

The fierce anger of a mother whose offspring was in danger erupted from her violently. Her bonds could not stop her getting at the surgeon. As they broke, she got up and dived for her baby on the trolley. The machine exploded in the surgeon's face. He screamed as his face blew away in tatters of blood and flesh and his body fell to the floor in a heap, smoking like his machine. She picked up her child and held it to her, its blood-covered form staining the whiteness of the gown she wore; she cried like a new mother should and held it tight to her protectively. She fell to her knees, holding it lovingly, glad that she was not alone now, glad that she had done something right in her life, something positive.

She got up and moved to the plastic door where strobe lights gleamed through and music blared. She went through and entered some club she had never been in before. There were no dancers, only girls like herself in surgical gowns. They were weeping on their knees and against the walls, while hundreds of aborted foetuses lay on the floor, screaming through partly formed mouths, screaming in torment and agony at their denied births.

Lou shrieked and fell to her knees again, still clutching the baby protectively to her. She collapsed to the floor hugging her foetus as her mind could not take any more horror. Then she shut herself off from the sights around her and her vision saw only darkness...

A pulsing strobe startled her waking eyes as she looked up at the ravers in the club. I'm still in Zeppelins! her mind cried thankfully. I'm still here! She rested against the wall and felt her stomach instinctively. It had changed now, she was sure; maybe it was just her imagination but her womb felt different now – changed. Dex! Her brother was in trouble. She had to help him. She ignored her womb and tried to get up, stumbling until she stood upright and looked over to where she had last seen her brother.

Dex looked down at the two people who had attacked him. Their veins were starting to pulsate and stretch against the skin. He knew what would happen next. And it did. A fountain of blood and hallucinogen sprayed upwards into his face, soaked into the skin, into his eyes, leaching into his mind and body. His vision went blood-red and all around him seemed to slowly disappear, fading away. Then the real horror came.

Chapter Twelve

De-birth in Pandemonium

Everything was red, blood-red. The whole club was covered in blood, it dripped from the walls and the ceiling. Bodies lay all over the floor and a deathly silence hung in the air: no music, not a sound. Needles protruded from the bodies that lay strewn across the dance floor – arms, legs, even penises – making a collection of collapsed veins, while by the walls a number of hospital beds stood with Ecstasy victims sprawled across them, drips and other assorted medical equipment hanging loose and useless to the floor. Dex wanted to be sick, the horror of the sight welled up inside him, bubbling away. This was sick, totally sick. Flies began to swarm, buzzing around and feeding on the decaying, overdosed corpses, settling around track marks, lips, scars and on urine-stained clothes. The buzz of their wings became louder and louder in Dex's ears until they started to hurt. He could feel the pressure build up in them with the increase of the sound of buzzing. But the smell... the smell was far worse... the stench of rotting flesh and stale urine invaded his senses, making his skin crawl and his stomach turn over and over as he tried to creep away from the scene.

'*Stop it! Stop it!*' he cried out, until his voice became a whisper due to the strain on his vocal cords.

And there amid the disgusting parade of death were the two people who had caused this nightmare, the two people he had just seen wither away like vampires in sunlight before him, before he himself had descended into this horror show. Their shaded lenses had cracked into fragments and their limbs collapsed until they fell to the floor a mass of bone and flesh side by side, screaming silently to themselves. Then, out of each of them, serpents emerged from their remains and slithered away over the corpses towards the doors.

Suddenly things began to change. Flashing colours strobed his eyeballs, and then, as if someone had switched on the club's sound system at full volume, a blast of thumping soundtrack pumped into his ears and all around him, its beat finding its way into him, his head and his body, until his entire anatomy was under its control. He jerked at its entrance. The silence of before now passed away as the beat animated him from the sickness of before; the colours he saw corresponded to the beat of the music, hypnotic and kaleidoscopic, like some psychedelic dream. It was like watching a television screen, the picture buzzing with electricity.

Something started to form from these dizzying colours: fingers, human fingers, then a wrist, and finally a whole arm, then dozens of them emerging from the colours, moving and stretching to the music. A shape started to form from the forearms, something emerging from where the veins would be: a cylinder shape, then a plunger on top, then a thin needle attaching it to the arm. The cylinders turned red and started to crack. The images of the over-dosed corpses returned to his mind to sicken him once again as the cracking blood-red vials began to shake until there was a shattering of exploding glass, tripled in sound in Dex's ears; and now he felt warm, poisoned junkie-blood splash his face, staining the skin, finding a way into every orifice: his nostrils, his ears, his mouth, his eye-sockets. The blood, contaminated with narcotics, stung him inside

and outside his head. His screaming was pointless; the
stinging felt like a thousand wasps around his head. He
tried to tear himself away from the music, but the beat
pounded deeper and deeper into his skull until it shook.

'*What more? What more?*'

'No more.'

A voice, somewhere in this madness. A soulful voice
bringing calm to this pandemonium. The voice of some
female angel. She then appeared through the colours,
dressed in a white Lycra dancing outfit, her blonde hair
shining as if with some light of holiness.

The colours he saw began to fade in their multitudes
and the music slowly faded into a background noise,
becoming almost inaudible. He could not believe this. An
image of calm and peace appeared before him, making his
penis stiffen with fantasised erotica.

'What more?' she asked. 'What do you mean?'

He gulped and looked at her.

'The horrors! The fucking horrors!'

Her hands caressed him, loosening his clothes until they
dropped to the floor.

'What would you like to do with me?' she asked,
unzipping the fly of her white shorts, revealing herself to
him. She was gorgeous. A dream woman. His erection said
it all.

'Come on then. Literally,' she said through red, pouting
lips. 'Fuck me like all the others…'

The images of all the girls he had been with plagued his
memory, flashing in a demented order through his
traumatised brain: the first names, the faces, the bodies.
Everything in his hedonistic past – lager, girls, driving,
lager, girls, driving, lager, girls, driving…

'Fuck me then!' The rave-angel was now a whore.

He roared as he broke away from the bonds of his
paralysis and shock, grabbing her and ripping away her

clothes from her body, pinning her to the ground, forcing himself into her, deeper and harder each time until she began to disintegrate before him, turning into a pile of powder. It exploded in his face and he fell back choking on it, snorting up into his nostrils. It was cocaine. He sneezed and coughed, trying to rid himself of it; he felt choked as he fell into it, the narcotic powder in his saliva, lining his mouth, tingling and irritating.

'Fucking coke-head!' said a voice.

He looked up, his face covered with the white powder. It was the rave-angel/whore again. He tried to block out her image, her voice. But he saw her in his mind and her voice rang in his ears. And all the time his erection grew harder, swelling and swelling to the point of ejaculation.

'What do you want with *me*?' he cried through lips caked with coke.

Then he ejaculated. But the smell was different; it was familiar and it burned his urethra as it left his testicles. It was pure alcohol. She laughed. From the lips of an angel came the mocking laugh of a demon. He felt a deep sickness, now, replacing the revulsion he had felt earlier.

Then a lightening flash of a strobe light blinded his eyes, a jolt that took him elsewhere...

...into the back seat of a car. A familiar car. Not his car; his parents' car. The old car. He was strapped into the back seat, his parents in front, his dad driving. He was speeding, getting faster and faster: forty, fifty, sixty, seventy –

'*Dad*!' he cried.

He was unheard.

Eighty, ninety –

His dad turned to face him, anger on his face. But it was not his father's face. It was his own. He himself was driving the car, with a feeling familiar to him – speed. The face turned away and continued its look of speeding determination. Then Dex saw the lorry. Not again! He had

been young then, too young. Dex's most painful memory...
Dad's death.

'*Daaaddddd!*'

Then the impact. Mum turned her head away; the straps
which held Dex cut into him. The windscreen imploded as
the bonnet was crushed in a scream of tearing metal. Glass
shards imploded upon the occupants, slicing into Dad's
face. His neck snapped forward, the seat belt cutting against
his body. Mum's face caught part of the glass, blood
streaking her face. Then the car stopped. Wrecked. Dad was
impaled on the steering wheel; Mum lay in a twisted
position in her seat. All went black for them, but not for
Dex.

A womb. A massive womb, pulsating with life. Then a
horrifying image of a young couple being eaten by something. Then the womb again. The close-up of what was
eating the couple – a huge yellow acid face with red eyes
and razor-sharp teeth. Then the womb again, glowing more
and more. Then the couple, flesh being torn away by the
razor teeth, blood emerging.

He wanted to scream. The image of the couple left him,
replaced by the womb again, a large image of hope and
survival. It pulsated with renewed energy, now; like a
beacon it shone in the blackness that surrounded it.

'*Mmmoooottthhheeeeerrrr!*'

He and she, his assailants, were regressing back to child-
like forms, then babies, their lenses slipping away to reveal
shining bright white eyes that looked like stars in the
blackness. They were caught in some vacuum, a force
sucking them back into their mother's womb. Dex
watched, his emotions in turmoil and tears streaming down
his face as they finally reverted, mother and babies together
for eternity. Then a bright light, a blinding white light,
seared his eyeballs: a light of hope.

'Dex...?'

Lou fought her way through the panicking clubbers, some of them bloodstained and hallucinating. One of them grabbed her, feeling her between the legs. She kneed him in the groin, and then when he was on the ground gave him a boot in the head. Violence was not part of her nature, but when needed, it flared up easily. She found Dex, on the floor covered in blood, tears mixing with the blood on his face. She knelt by him and shook him.

'Dex...?'

No answer.

'*Dex*! Come out of it you bastard!'

'Dex...'

He heard his name being called, a distant voice in the blackness. The womb was gone; only himself was left now. Then another light began to appear, melting away the blackness.

'Dex!'

A face started to emerge.

'Dex! Come out of it...'

The words were lost, trailing into the new light. A familiar face started to emerge from the light, looming over his own. He was shaking. He was being shaken. He recognised the face. Lou.

'*Come on!*' she grabbed him, shaking him violently.

Still no response.

'*Come on!*'

His head now started to bang against the floor. Then his lips quivered, starting to form words.

'Lou...' His voice was a whisper under the still pounding bass.

She nearly cried, but grabbed him instead, gripping the T-shirt he wore, dragging him to his feet.

'We've got to get out of here!' she shouted in his ear.

He nodded dumbly, his senses slowly coming back to him, his feet wobbling on the dance floor, bumping into other escaping clubbers looking for the exit.

They fought their way out into the open, stumbling away from the pandemonium inside. The fresh night air hit them, bringing Dex closer to sobriety and they fell against a wall and slid to the floor, exhausted. Tears pricked at Lou's eyes when she looked down at the shape that was Dex, bloodstained and shattered. The tears began to flow now, as she realised that she had almost lost another member of her family.

She felt her stomach, sensing the baby that was starting to form there, starting to grow into another human being. There was hope after this madness, she thought. It was inside her, a whole new life, a change for the better. She looked upwards into the star-speckled night sky and new change was already here. Things were going to be better now, for the good.

Chapter Thirteen
End of the Era

The emergency services swarmed into the club. Music was still banging away and there were people all over the place, some being sick, others comatose, others wandering aimlessly amid the chaos. If they thought the bloodstained victims were the worst cases, they had yet to see what was waiting in the centre of the dance floor. The first paramedic doubled up and vomited at the sight. Others crowded round to see the sight: two dead bodies in a pool of their own blood and liquids – one male, one female.

The bodies of two babies.